!
Ahoy!
0010
00111
?
Hi!
Hello!

COMICS LAND

by
CAPSTONE

capstone
www.capstoneyoungreaders.com

1710 Roe Crest Drive, North Mankato, Minnesota 56003

Cataloging-in-Publication data is available on the Library of Congress website.
ISBN: 978-1-4342-6285-1 (hardcover) • ISBN: 978-1-4342-4989-0 (library binding) •
ISBN: 978-1-4342-6432-9 (eBook)

Printed in China by Nordica. 0413/CA21300502 032013 007226NORDF13

MY LITTLE BRO-BOT

written by
AMY & DONALD LEMKE

illustrated by
JESS BRADLEY

designed by
BOB LENTZ

edited by
JULIE GASSMAN

A few years ago, my brother was born in Comics Land Hospital.
goo
goo
goo
goo
goo
goo
goo
goo

And I was going to be the best big sister EVER!
Gimme! Gimme!
I'll always take care of you...
...my little Bro-Bot.

And I did...I fed him.
Are you hungry, Bro-Bot?
Honey Nuts + Bolts!
Honey Nuts Bolts
POUR
Num num num num
I changed his leaky diapers.
TINK TINK
TINK
Oopie!
There you go, Bro-Bot! All dry.

I oiled his rusty rashes.
Don't worry, Bro-Bot. I'll fix it.
SQUEAK
SQUEAK
SQUEAK
There you go, Bro-Bot. Good as new.
DRIP
DRIP

And with my help, he grew...
S-
BB-
And grew...
BB-
BB-
And grew...
BB-
BB-

And GREW!
BB—
BB
BB
S
BB

Until one day...
Have fun at the park, you two. Keep an eye on your Bro-Bot.
Take my hand, little Bro-Bot.
I'm a big robot now. Big robots do not need help.

You heard Mom! Give me your hand, Bro-Bot.
No, Sam. I can do it.
CLICK!
BRO-BOT!
KRRRRRRRRR

AH!!
FWOOSH
Stop, Bro-Bot! Turn your rocket boosters off!
NOW!
BEEEEP!

PUTT
PUTT
PUTT
Uh-oh.
AHHHHHHH
CRASH!

Where are we?
And just how are we supposed to get home?
Don't worry, Sam.
Big robots always know their way.
BEEP!

Follow me, sis.

Good grief.

An hour later...
Are you sure you don't want my help?
NO! Big robots never get lost.
But I am a little hungry.

Sure, Bro-Bot.
LOOK
LOOK
SEARCH
Here you go!
HONEY NUTS & BOLTS!
yum!
Rocket Booster
Win!
CLINK
Num num num num

Many hours later...
How about now, Bro-Bot? Would you like some help?
No, thank you. Big robots are not afraid.
BEEP!

Oopie.
But I am a little wet.
There you go, Bro-Bot! All dry.
Then let's keep going.

Many, many hours later...
And now would you like some help, Bro-Bot?
Nope. Big robots do not get tired.
RUSTLE
RUSTLE

SQUEAK
SQUEAK

But I am a little rusty.
There you go, Bro-Bot.
Good as new.
DRIP

And soon...
LOOK, Bro-Bot! Over there!
We're home.
I told you, Sam.

You were right. Big robots don't need any help.
No, they don't.
But they always need their big sister.
And I'll always need you.
END!

Elsewhere in COMICS LAND...
Why is this cowboy surrounded by monkeys?

And how did these monkeys go from being tied up...

...to tying up the cowboy and horse?!

Find out in the pages of...

only in

COMICS LAND

by CAPSTONE

My Little Bro-Bot Presents

GAME TIME!

Every box, balloon, and burst in a comic has a special name and job. Can you match the object with its name?

A. SOUND BURST

B. SURPRISE LINES

C. EXCITEMENT BALLOON

D. WORD BALLOON

E. MOTION LINES

F. SOUND EFFECT

G. NARRATIVE BOX

H. THOUGHT BALLOON

1=D, 2=H, 3=G, 4=A, 5=E, 6=B, 7=F, 8=C

Unscramble the letters to reveal words from the story.

1. HOERRBT	5. SRACH
2. BROOT	6. UNHYGR
3. PREADIS	7. YTRUS
4. TRECOK	8. RSTEIS

1. BROTHER, 2. ROBOT, 3. DIAPERS, 4. ROCKET, 5. CRASH, 6. HUNGRY, 7. RUSTY, 8. SISTER

FIND THE NUTS!

With all of Sam and Bro-Bot's adventures, some of Bro-Bot's bolts have lost their nuts! Look at the story again to search and find **11** gold-colored nuts in all!

MY LITTLE BRO-BOT

PRESENTS

DRAW COMICS!

Want to make your own comic about Sam and Bro-Bot? Start by learning to draw the robot. Comics Land artist Jess Bradley shows you how in six easy steps!

You will need:

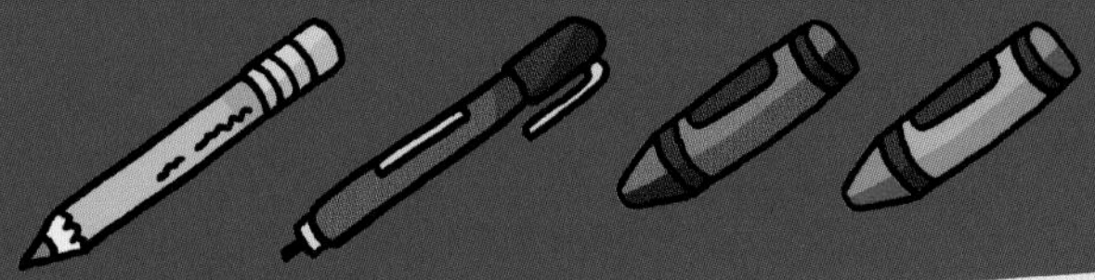

3.

4.

5.

Outline in ink!

6.

Color!

AMY & DONALD LEMKE

AUTHORS

Amy and Donald Lemke are a husband-and-wife team from Hugo, Minnesota. When not caring for their baby girl, fending off their golden retriever, or shooing away their cat, they manage to write a few books. In addition, Donald is a children's book editor and freelance writer, with works published by Capstone, HarperCollins, Running Press, and more. Amy is an Early Childhood Special Education teacher and writer.

JESS BRADLEY

ARTIST

Jess Bradley is an illustrator living and working in Bristol, England. She likes playing video games, painting, and watching bad films. Jess can also be heard to make a high-pitched "squeeeee" when excited, usually while watching videos clips of otters or getting new comics in the mail.

Hoo!
BEANS!
Later!
See you next time!
SQUEE!